the Swan princess™

Adapted by David Buchanan

From the film by Richard Rich

MAMMOTH

First published in 1995 by Mammoth
an imprint of Reed Children's Books
Michelin House, 81 Fulham Road, London SW3 6RB
and Auckland, Melbourne, Singapore and Toronto

The Swan Princess copyright © 1994 by Nest Productions, Inc.
Licensed through Leisure Concepts, Inc.
All rights reserved

Line illustrations by Emilie Kong Studios
Copyright © 1994 by Nest Productions Inc.

ISBN 0 7497 2028 X

A CIP catalogue record for this title is available from the British Library

Printed and bound in Great Britain
by Cox & Wyman Ltd, Reading, Berks

1

"Odette."

King William smiled at the sleeping baby in his arms. Again he whispered, "Odette."

Odette would be his daughter's name. It meant wealthy, and that is how he felt in his heart. King William had ruled the land with wisdom and kindness for many years. He had riches beyond imagination, and his subjects loved him, but in spite of that, William had been sad and lonely, for he did not have a child. By the time he was sixty he had all but given up hope.

And then Odette had come.

He cradled the tiny girl in his arms, then he carried her toward the royal balcony. Two beaming servants flung open the glass doors. Outside, the entire kingdom waited for his news. With tears in his eyes, King William held his daughter up for all to see. "Long live Princess Odette!" he cried.

"LONG LIVE THE PRINCESS!" replied his subjects. Their cry could be heard in the next kingdom.

For weeks afterwards, kings and queens arrived to greet the child and all marvelled at the baby's beauty. Each day the castle was crowded with courtiers. On one such day the widowed Queen Uberta came with her small son, Derek. Prince Derek ran up to Odette's cradle. He looked inside. Ugh! he thought. A baby! He dropped a golden locket into the cradle, just as his mother had told him to. Done it, he thought. Now I can go home.

He turned around. Everyone in the room was smiling at him, except for King William and his mother, who were smiling at each other. In their minds, they were planning Derek's marriage to Odette.

But hidden among the visitors that day was a red-haired old man. The baby princess meant nothing to him. His threatening eyes darted around the room. This will all be mine some day, he thought. The room, the castle, the entire kingdom.

His name was Rothbart, and he was an enchanter with an evil plan. By mastering the Forbidden Arts, he would gain the power to take King William's kingdom. Day and night he practised his sorcery in a secret lair, with only the help of his loyal Hag.

News of Rothbart's plan reached King William and on the eve of his attack, the king sent his army to destroy the Enchanter's hiding place. Rothbart and the Hag were brought before King William.

"Death to the Enchanter!" cried the people of the kingdom.

But King William, as always, showed mercy.

"I will not take a life," he announced, "but I hereby banish Rothbart from my kingdom forever."

Rothbart was far from grateful.

"I'm not finished with you yet, Willie," he growled as he was dragged away. "Someday I'll get my power back. And when I do, everything you own, everything you love, will be mine!"

2

Queen Uberta's chamberlain tried to blow the royal
trumpet, but no sound came out. He peered out
into the distance from a high turret of the castle.
Yes, without a doubt that was King William's
caravan approaching. Today was to be the first
meeting between the young Prince Derek and
Princess Odette!

King William and Princess Odette entered the
castle. Queen Uberta received them with open
arms, but beside her Prince Derek frowned. Derek
remembered putting the locket into Odette's cradle.
He was five now, but she was only just three. He
wanted nothing to do with her.

"Dear Uberta," the King said. "As lovely as ever."

"And who might this strapping young man be?"
he said, patting Derek on the head. "Young Prince
Derek, no doubt."

"Welcome to our fair kingdom, dear William,"
said Queen Uberta, "and to you, young Princess."

The king nudged his daughter forward. Her
golden locks bobbed up and down as she walked
toward Derek.

How horrible! thought Derek.

"Go on, Derek!" Uberta whispered.

"Mother!" Derek whined.

Queen Uberta looked disapprovingly at him. "Derek!"

Derek reluctantly stepped forward and said very quickly, "Hello-Princess-Odette-I-am-very-pleased-to-meet-you."

Odette smiled shyly. "Hello," she said.

Derek turned away but his mother stopped him with a warning look. Derek had almost forgotten. This was the worst part of all. He knelt down and quickly kissed Odette's hand.

King William and Queen Uberta beamed. There was hope, or so they thought.

Every summer the king and queen brought their children together, but Odette was not happy to see Derek, and Derek did not like Odette. For several years, they tormented each other mercilessly. Then Derek made friends with a boy of his own age, Bromley and after that the boys ganged up on Odette.

A nobleman, Lord Rogers, was Derek's tutor. Under the queen's instructions, he taught the boy how to behave. But Derek went on teasing Odette and she fought back. Outsmarting Bromley was no problem, but Derek was another story. She and he were a good match, but not the kind of match their parents had in mind.

At last Odette reached the age of sixteen. Across the land, she was admired for her intelligence, beauty and grace.

Prince Derek had grown into a brave, honest and intelligent lad, gifted with the bow and arrow. But Queen Uberta and King William had long since despaired of their children ever liking each other.

When Odette's carriage arrived at the castle gate, Odette was not looking forward to seeing Derek. As usual Derek squirmed impatiently, thinking about target practice, lunch, horse-riding, anything but that stupid, silly girl.

But when Derek went in to meet Odette in the ballroom, his heart began to thump like a galloping horse, and her smile made him weak at the knees. She had the same face, hair and eyes as Odette, but seemed to be someone quite different.

"Hello, Derek," Odette said.

Derek could hardly speak. Could this be the same girl? he wondered.

Derek returned Odette's smile. He held out his arm, and Odette took it. Together they walked onto the dance floor as music began to play. Derek was so happy, he felt he was dancing on air.

Queen Uberta almost fainted with joy.

During the rest of that summer, Derek and Odette spent all their time together. They went riding through the palace gardens and hardly ever left each other's side.

Derek dreamed of Odette. He awoke each morning eager to see her. When he was with her he felt overjoyed, but he was tongue-tied and could not tell her how he felt.

How could I ever have hated her? he wondered. Hate was the furthest thing from his mind now, for he could not imagine ever living without her.

When the summer was over, on the day Odette was to leave, the couple danced all night at a royal ball. Lord Rogers conducted the royal orchestra and William and Uberta watched and waited. No one at the ball could mistake the love that burned in the eyes of Odette and Derek. As they whirled across the dance floor, swept up in their emotions, all the guests stopped to admire them.

Odette smiled at her handsome prince, but inside she felt a tug of sadness. She couldn't bear to leave him. In his shy way Derek had given her so much love over the summer, but he had never declared it. Maybe he would tonight. Maybe he'd finally tell her how he felt.

For the last dance of the night, Lord Rogers brought the orchestra to a rousing finish. Queen Uberta prepared to bid the guests good-bye. Derek and Odette stopped dancing. They shared a long glance. Then Derek turned to the guests with an enormous, joyous grin. At the top of his voice, he blurted out: "Arrange the wedding!"

The noise suddenly stopped. Queen Uberta and King William were speechless.

But in that moment of silence, Odette called out, "Wait!"

Cries of happiness caught in the guests' throats and the ballroom remained silent.

"What is it?" Derek pleaded. "You're all I ever wanted. You're beautiful!"

"Thank you," Odette replied. "But – what else?"

Surely Derek wanted more than her beauty? In her soul, Odette knew Derek loved her as much as she loved him. All she needed was for him to say it.

He could whisper it to her, or declare it before the kingdom. But he stared at her blankly. "What else?" he repeated.

"Is beauty all that matters to you?" Odette asked.

King William and Queen Uberta stood, dumbfounded.

Derek swallowed hard. "I . . . er . . . what else is there?" he said.

Odette's heart sank. She had been wrong, she thought. Derek did not love her at all. She turned to leave the ballroom, taking the hopes of two kingdoms with her.

The following day, as a crestfallen King William led his daughter away, Derek and Odette barely said goodbye.

Derek watched the king's caravan depart, his eyes red with shock and bitter disappointment.

His mother could offer no comfort. Her smile of farewell gave way to a look of despair.

"All these years of planning, wasted!" she murmured.

She turned away and left her son alone with his grief.

3

"What else is there?" Lord Rogers said the words mockingly as he paced the royal sitting room. "She says, 'Is beauty all that matters?' and you say, 'What else is there?'"

"It was dumb, I know," Derek replied.

Candles flickered against the growing darkness outside. The rain, pelting against the windows, was not helping Derek's mood.

"You should write a book," Rogers continued, "'How to Offend Women in Five Syllables or Less.'"

"Think!" urged Rogers. "You must see something other than Odette's beauty."

"Of course I do, Rogers!" Derek said.

"She's . . . well, you know. And then, well . . . er. . ."

Lord Rogers rolled his eyes.

"Oh, I just don't know how to say it!" Derek finally blurted out, and then he added, "I know, I'll prove it to her. I'll prove my love!"

Miles away in a dark secluded forest, an old man waited behind an oak tree. His eyes were trained on King William's caravan, plodding slowly along the mud-soaked trail.

"Today's the day, Willie," Rothbart whispered, staring at King William's coach. "Everything you own, everything you love, will be mine!"

The rain did not bother Rothbart. He had worked these sixteen years to regain his magical powers, and nothing could stop him now.

Inside the royal carriage, King William shook his head sadly.

"I just don't understand," he said to his daughter. "What else did you want him to say?"

"I need to know that he loves me," Odette replied.

Suddenly the horses whinnied and bucked, and the carriage lurched to a stop.

"What on earth – ?" King William turned the door handle and stepped out. Beyond the horses, a caped man was blocking the path. Although the man was in silhouette, King William recognized the aggressive stance and hunched posture. Could it really be Rothbart, after all these years?

"Stay inside, Odette," he warned, closing the carriage door.

The king took a step forward. His guards moved to encircle him, spears drawn.

Rothbart opened his arms. A fireball of light exploded around him. His cape became a pair of leathery black wings, his fingers sharp talons.

Shielding their eyes, the king and his guards stepped backward. Before them stood a hideous bird-like animal.

It attacked with a deafening roar.

A door creaked. Derek, Bromley and Lord Rogers turned at the noise. Who could be pushing open the castle door at this hour? With a dull wet thump, a man slumped onto the floor. His uniform was ripped and muddy, his face covered with bruises.

"It's King William's Captain!" Derek cried.

He ran to the man and propped up his head while Rogers and Bromley rushed to his side.

The captain struggled to speak. "We - we were attacked," he said, his voice a parched whisper. "A Great Animal . . ."

Derek looked up and exclaimed, "Odette!"

He set the captain down gently and made for the door.

"No, Derek!" Lord Rogers shouted after him. "Wait!"

But Derek ignored him. He raced to the royal stable, jumped on his horse and took off. The horse sent up clods of mud as it galloped through the forest. Derek blinked away raindrops and trained his eyes on the path. Deep in the woods he spotted the twisted wreckage of a caravan. He brought the horse to a halt and jumped off.

Carriage wheels were strewn about, surrounded by a jumble of splintered carriages.

"Odette?" he cried, pulling open a carriage door. It was empty.

He heard a voice behind him moaning and spun around. Lying against an overturned wagon was King William, bruised and exhausted. The king's eyes flickered open as Derek rushed to his side.

"Who did this?" Derek said, holding King William's head in his lap.

"It came - so quickly," the king struggled to say. "A Great Animal . . ."

"Where is Odette?" Derek pleaded.

"Listen to me, Derek," said King William in a faint whisper. "It's not what it seems. It's not what it seems."

"What's not what it seems? Where is Odette?"

"Odette . . ." The king winced with pain, and murmured, "Odette . . . has . . . been . . .taken. "

King William's closed his eyes.

Derek threw back his head and let out a cry of anguish, the cry of a boy who has lost everything.

"ODETTE!"

In a remote dark corner of the forest, the moon
began to rise over a decrepit castle. Although the
rain had stopped, water ran from the crumbling
turrets and gables

Attached to this castle was a tall water dungeon,
surrounded by a moat. Beyond that was a stone
floor ending in a set of stone stairs that led
downward to a lake, on which a lonely swan glided.

Rothbart and the Hag happily tossed bread
crumbs to the majestic white bird.

"Don't let my little spell make you sad, Odette,"
Rothbart said. "It doesn't last the whole day. As
soon as the moon comes up . . ."

He didn't need to finish. Creeping across the lake, the moonlight touched the swan's wing. Water began to swirl up from below. The swan rose upward in a shimmering geyser of light and transformed into Princess Odette.

"And that's how it works every night," Rothbart said, as Odette landed gently on the shore. "You have to be on the lake, of course, and when the moonlight touches your wings you're human!"

Odette turned away from him. All she could think

about was her father. She would never forgive Rothbart for what he had done.

"Look, Odette," Rothbart went on, "this sort of thing doesn't give me any pleasure, well, maybe a teeny bit, but what I really want is your father's kingdom."

"With all your power, why don't you just take it?" Odette retorted.

"I've tried that already, but once you steal something, you spend your whole life fighting to keep it." Rothbart moved closer. "But if I marry the only heir to the throne, we can rule together as king and queen!"

Odette couldn't believe her ears. "Never!"

She shoved him aside and marched off angrily toward the forest.

Rothbart laughed. "Where are you going? As soon as the moonlight leaves the lake, you'll turn back into a swan wherever you are!"

Odette stopped. On foot she would never make it out of the forest in time. She was his prisoner.

Hidden behind a nearby tree, a frog and a turtle watched sadly.

"Looks like she's going to be here for a while, Speed," said the frog.

"Poor girl," groaned the turtle.

Meanwhile, Prince Derek searched through the wreckage, but found no sign of Odette. Could she be alive? Was she being held a prisoner? Who or what was the Great Animal? He vowed to hunt the creature down.

He barely slept that night, and at sunrise ordered Lord Rogers to arrange a royal target practice. The court musicians, dressed as animals, ran through the woods and tried to avoid being hit. Derek and Bromley used soft, harmless arrows, each with a powder-puff tip. Derek's arrows were dipped in orange powder, Bromley's in blue, to leave a mark for each hit.

Derek did not miss a shot and was the winner.

"You're a great marksman, Derek," Bromley said, putting his arm around his friend's shoulder. "But it takes more than good aim. It takes courage. That's my forte."

Behind them, Lord Rogers called out, "Well then, how about a quick round of Catch and Fire?"

Bromley's face turned green. "Catch and Fire? Me?"

"You're the only one with enough courage," Rogers said with a smile.

Bromley had never tried Catch and Fire. He had hoped he never would, but now he would have to.

Rogers and Derek disappeared into the castle armoury and returned with two bows, one arrow, a suit of armour, a shield and an apple. Shaking with fear, Bromley put on the armour and picked up the bow and arrow. Rogers placed the apple on top of Bromley's helmet. Across the field, Derek stood with a shield of armour at his back. He turned away from Bromley. Bromley lifted his bow and aimed an arrow at Derek's back.

"What if I – ?" he whimpered.

"Remember, now, aim for the heart," Rogers replied calmly. "Right between the shoulders."

"Oh, please not – please not . . ." Bromley pleaded. He stretched the arrow back and let fly. "Now!" he cried as the arrow flew toward Derek. Derek whirled around, and in one move grabbed the flying arrow, loaded it into his own bow and shot it back. Bromley closed his eyes and gritted his teeth. Above his head, the arrow split the apple neatly in two.

Bromley's knees buckled and he fell to the ground. Lord Rogers caught a chunk of apple and took a bite. "Well done, Derek!" he cried.

But Derek was gazing into the distant forest.

"Hold on, Odette," he said under his breath. "I'm going to find you."

6

"Quiet!" said Jean-Bob, the frog. "I can't concentrate."

Speed, the turtle, tried not to laugh as Jean-Bob took hold of the long chain of bulrushes and prepared to pole-vault. He could hop great distances by himself, but not all the way across the moat to the tall tower, Rothbart's water dungeon.

At the base of the tower, in a clump of mud above the water line, grew the most perfect flowers Jean-Bob had ever seen. For the Princess, he would risk his life to snatch those flowers. He would even vault above the heads of the hungry alligators.

"You've come up with some daft ideas, Jean-Bob," Speed said, "but this one is really mad."

Jean-Bob dusted himself off.

"Go ahead and laugh," he said, picking some more bulrushes off the ground. "I'll get that princess to kiss me, and when she does – "

"You'll change into a prince," Speed finished. "I know, I know, you've told me."

"When she learns zat I have risked my life for zose flowers, ze kissing will not stop!" Jean-Bob smiled as he attached three strong bulrushes together.

Speed had heard Jean-Bob's frog prince story a hundred times. He'd given up telling Jean-Bob how ridiculous it sounded.

"Mind if I point out a problem?" Speed asked.

"I don't take advice from peasants," Jean-Bob sniffed.

"Suit yourself," Speed replied.

Jean-Bob balanced his bulrush pole. He hunched over, closed his eyes, and chanted softly. "Flowers, kiss, concentration. Flowers, kiss, concentration." Then, opening his eyes, he ran toward the moat.

He planted the pole and leaped. Up over the moat he sailed.

"I'm a bit curious about how you're going to get back," Speed called out.

Jean-Bob's eyes went wide. Below him, the teeth of two alligators gleamed. The pole was taking him down, down, down where an alligator was snapping at him. It was so close, Jean-Bob could smell the bad breath.

"Aaagh!" he shrieked.

The pole now sprang him back to dry land.

"Help! Speed! Stop me!" Jean-Bob pleaded.

Speed inched forward and tried to grab Jean-Bob,

but in vain. Back he went towards the water. The alligators swooped, just as the bulrush sprang the frog back to land.

"Help! Help me!" Jean-Bob cried.

Back and forth he swung, dropping closer and closer to the waiting jaws. He closed his eyes. He wasn't moving. He was still. He opened his eyes. A gasp caught in his throat.

Odette herself was holding the tip of the bulrush in her hand. She had stopped the swinging, and she was smiling at him!

"Odette!" Jean-Bob exclaimed. He jumped off the bulrush and bowed. "Oh, thank you, thank you!"

"What in the world were you trying to do?" asked Odette.

Speed chuckled. "He thought that if – "

"Shush!" Jean-Bob snapped. Then, chin raised high, he said to Odette, "I wanted to get zose flowers for you."

Odette raised a suspicious eyebrow. "You're being sneaky again, Jean-Bob."

"Sneaky? Me? You deserve a nice bouquet."

"And you deserve a kiss?"

Jean-Bob offered his cheek. "Well, all right. If you insist."

"Give it up, Jean-Bob," Speed remarked.

Odette smiled at Jean-Bob.

"You know I'm under a spell," she said.

"But my kiss will break ze spell!" Jean-Bob insisted.

Odette shook her head.

"I can only kiss the man I love, and then he . . ."

"Must make a vow of everlasting love," Jean-Bob cut in.

"And prove it to the world!" Odette added.

"What do you think I was doing with ze flowers and ze alligators, going back and forth? Everlasting love!" Jean-Bob sniffed indignantly. "I was almost everlasting lunch!"

A sudden crash stopped their conversation. Lying on the ground a few yards away, an arrow jutting from its wing, was a black-and-white bird. Odette, Jean-Bob and Speed gathered around it.

"Do you think he's dead?" Speed asked.

"No," Odette answered. "It's just his wing, I think."

"Strange-looking bird," Jean-Bob remarked.

"Poor fellow," Odette said. "He must be in a lot of pain."

Tenderly she examined the bird's injured wing.

With a quick snap, Odette broke the arrow. Then, gingerly, she pulled it out. Tearing a strip of cloth from her dress, she wrapped it around the wing. Slowly the bird's eyes opened. At first he thought he was under attack. The bird stood, ready to fight.

"Ha! It takes more than a pair of pond punks to keep Puffin down! Ha!" he snapped.

"But I'm your friend!" Odette said.

Once he realised that Odette had removed the

arrow from his wing the bird bowed.

"In that case, please accept my apology. My name is Puffin. Lieutenant Puffin."

"It's a pleasure. I'm Odette. Princess Odette."

Odette held out her hand, and Puffin kissed it.

"And these are my best friends in the whole world," Odette continued. "Mister Lorenzo Trudgealong – "

"Friends call me Speed," Speed said.

"And Jean-Bob."

Jean-Bob bowed deeply. "I have no friends, only servants, and they call me 'Your Highness'."

He held out his hand to be kissed.

"He thinks he's a prince," Speed explained.

"Well!" Puffin said, ignoring Jean-Bob. "I'm in your debt, Princess, and I'll stay until my debt is paid."

"I don't think there's much you can do," Odette replied. "Rothbart the Enchanter has me under a spell."

"You mean, a magical – " Puffin waved his wings.

In an instant, the dark forest became bright as day. The gnarled trees bloomed with cherry blossoms. Rothbart himself appeared in full armour, his helmet in his hand.

"Your knight in shining armour has come to set

you free!" he mocked.

Puffin stepped up to fight Rothbart, but Speed and Jean-Bob pulled him back.

"Let me at him!" Puffin shouted. "I'll – "

Speed squeezed Puffin's beak shut as Rothbart bent down on one knee.

"All it takes is one word, Odette. Will you marry me?" he sighed.

"Every night you ask the same question," Odette replied. "And every night I give you the same answer. I'll die first!"

Rothbart scowled.

"You're beginning to make me angry," Rothbart said.

He bit his finger to control his emotions. Then, practically spitting his words out, he said, "I was hoping you'd say you'd be mine, but it looks as if you need another day to think about it."

As Rothbart turned back toward his castle, Odette sank to the ground. She would never marry him! She would remain a swan forever if she had to. Burying her head in her hands, she burst into tears.

7

Uberta stood in the sunfilled Crown Room, talking to Lord Rogers.

"Soon Derek will be married and the kingdom will have a king again," Uberta said.

"I doubt it," Rogers replied. "Derek still refuses to be king unless he can find Odette."

"Poppycock! All that will change at tomorrow night's ball," the queen smiled confidently.

Suddenly the door flew open and the chamberlain barged in. He was smiling so hard, his chubby cheeks seemed ready to crack.

"They're all coming!" he said. "Every princess is coming!"

He turned toward the door and clapped his hands. Two servants stepped inside, each carrying a bulging mailbag.

Uberta ran to the chamberlain and took a handful of letters.

Replies, they were all replies, accepting her invitation!

"Oh, this is wonderful!" Uberta exclaimed, "You see, Rogers, one of these young ladies is bound to change Derek's mind."

"Oh, absolutely . . ." Rogers replied. To himself, he added, "Not."

"Now, where is Derek? Oh, I know! He's in the library, working on the mystery of the Fat Animal."

"The Great Animal, Your Highness," Rogers corrected her.

"Oh, Big, Great, Fat, whatever," the queen said. "It's large and it has fur."

In the library, Prince Derek climbed a ladder to the top book shelf. He pulled out a thick musty book and blew dust off the cover.

He read the title: *Beasts and Spirits of the Night*. This could be it, he thought. He began flipping through the pages. It's not what it seems. It's not what it seems. What had King William meant?

Finally his fingers stopped at a chapter entitled, 'Animal Transformations'. As he scanned through the pages, his face lit up.

"It's not what it seems – of course!" Quickly he ripped out a handful of pages and clutched them tightly. "Now I'll find you, Odette!"

He leaped off the ladder. His feet hit the floor near the library entrance and he came face to face with his mother.

"Oh!" Queen Uberta cried. She jumped back, dropping some of the letters she'd been carrying.

Derek spun her around and ran out of the library.

"Where are you going, Derek?" Uberta demanded.

"To find the Great Animal!" Derek replied,

waving the ripped-out pages high. "I've worked it out!"

"Wonderful. Just make sure you're here for tomorrow night."

"What?" Derek stopped and turned. "Tomorrow night?"

"The ball!" Uberta reminded him.

"Mother, I - I can't."

Uberta's face fell. Her eyes began to water.

"Please, Mother, don't cry!" said Derek impatiently.

Uberta controlled her tears, but her lower lip began to quiver.

"All right," sighed Derek. "If I leave now, maybe I can get back in time."

His mother broke into a huge smile, throwing the letters into the air with joy.

"But please, Mother, don't turn this into one of your big beauty pageants."

"Oh, no, no, no," Uberta insisted. "It's just a few friends . . ."

Derek nodded and dashed out of the library.

When he was out of sight, Uberta finished her sentence.

". . . and their daughters."

The chamberlain came huffing and puffing into

the room, scooping up letters.

"I want this ball to be big!" the queen exclaimed. "Every princess must have her own introduction."

"But you said – ," began Lord Rogers.

"Forget what I said! Now, send for the cooks and tell the band to start rehearsing. And I want four footmen for every carriage."

"Yes, Your Highness," the chamberlain bowed and scurried away.

At a campsite in the forest, Prince Derek threw down a page he had ripped out of his book. It was a picture of a mouse.

Bromley bit into an apple and examined the picture.

"It's a mouse," he said.

"No." Derek shook his head. "It's the Great Animal."

Bromley laughed. "A touch small, wouldn't you say?"

"Yes, until it changes into this." Derek laid out three more pictures. In each one, the mouse was larger and more hideous. In the last, it had taken on the shape of an enormous beast. Bromley

believed it. Derek was no fool. And with that
monster loose in the forest, Bromley was certainly
not going to leave Derek's side.

8

Puffin watched the last trace of the moon disappear behind the lake. He had just seen Princess Odette change into a swan, but he could hardly believe his eyes. The sleek white swan barely left a ripple in the still water as she swam.

"All she needs is a little moonlight," Jean-Bob said with a sigh. "All I need is to be kissed."

Puffin thought hard. There had to be a way. "I've got it!" he blurted out. "We'll find Derek and lure him back to the lake!"

The others stared at him blankly.

"We get here just as the moon is coming up," Puffin went on. "The Prince comes through the forest, you change into a Princess – happy ever after!"

As Puffin made final plans, Speed floated lazily on the lake. Jean-Bob lay on Speed's back, and Odette swam beside them.

On the shore, Puffin stood and cleared his throat. "Ahem! Attention!"

Odette and Speed snapped upright in the water and Jean-Bob leapt into the air.

"It's zero hour, troops!" Puffin shouted. "Odette,

prepare for takeoff!"

"Right," Odette replied.

"The rest of you have your assignments here, back on land," Puffin directed. "Is everyone ready?"

"Ready for action," they all cried.

"Take off!" Puffin bellowed.

Beating their wings mightily, he and Odette took to the air.

"Good luck," Speed said. "Have a nice flight!"

"Be careful," Jean-Bob called out. "If anything happens to her, I'll have you flogged, whipped, put on ze rack and zen have your legs fried in butter!"

Bromley was shaking. Derek and he were entering the forest now. Even in the daytime, the place was dark. And not only that, it was full of creatures, full of possible disguises for the Great Animal. Derek stole through the trees like a cat. Bromley stumbled behind, panting, looking for anything that might possibly be a disguise for the Great Animal.

High above the forest, Odette and Puffin flew steadily toward Derek's castle. Puffin's wing felt as strong as ever now, but Odette was nervous.

"You don't think there could be any hunters, do you?" she asked.

"Relax, Odette," Puffin replied. "I can smell a human a mile away."

Suddenly an arrow shot past so close that Odette could feel its breeze. She and Puffin both let out a scream.

"Where did that come from?" cried Puffin.

Then they both heard a shout, "DE-RRREK!"

Odette recognized the voice. It was Bromley's!

"Derek," she repeated. "He's here!"

"You will not lose control," Puffin commanded. "You will follow the plan as outlined."

But Odette wasn't listening. Desperately, her eyes searched the area below for any sign of her beloved.

Puffin flew under her, blocking her view. But Odette dodged him and dived downward.

"Odette!" Puffin called, racing after her.

Not far away, Bromley quietly lined up his prey along the shaft of his arrow. A mouse cowered against a rock, trapped.

"I've got you now!" Bromley gloated. "Don't give me that innocent look! Go ahead, transform! I'm not afraid of you!"

The mouse shivered with fright. He let out a tiny squeak.

Bromley dropped his bow and ran screaming into the woods. Derek didn't hear his friend's scream. He was concentrating. Above the treetops was a golden-white flash of light. It was moving toward him, shimmering as it passed around tangled branches. Quietly, quickly, he put an arrow to his bowstring and raised his bow, ready for the shot. From the sound of it, he'd have to be quick. He peered out from behind a tree and aimed. In his sight, flying toward him at great speed, was a majestic white bird.

Derek lowered his bow. A swan?

Of course, he said to himself. It's not what it seems. It's not what it seems! This was a trap. It had to be.

"Just a little closer," he murmured. "Come on. Come on . . ."

There. It was close enough now. He stepped out from the tree, lining the swan in his sight. With all his strength, he pulled the bowstring taut. This time he would not miss.

"This one," he announced out loud, "is for Odette!"

Derek let go. The arrow sliced the air, dead on target!

9

"Odette!"

The shout tore Puffin's throat. He hurtled downward, crashing into Odette. They bounced away from each other just as Derek's arrow shot between them, slicing branches off the trees. Odette regained her balance, then took to the sky. She beat her wings furiously, staring straight ahead.

"That was close!" Puffin said, struggling to catch up.

"We never planned that!" Odette replied.

Puffin looked down. He saw Derek racing after them, following their shadows.

"The plan is working!" Puffin cried out. "Here he comes!"

When he looked back up, Odette was far in front of him. Fear for her life propelled her forward and her mind was a jumble of frantic thoughts. Derek hadn't recognized her. But she hadn't expected him to. So why had she flown so close to him? Why hadn't she followed Puffin's plan to lure Derek back to the lake? Now he was after her. But why? Why did he want to shoot her? And what had he meant by saying 'This one's for Odette'?

Puffin glanced below and saw the top of Derek's head directly underneath them.

"Speed up, girl! That boy of yours can certainly move!"

"He's too close, Puffin!" Odette cried.

"Don't worry, Odette. I've been taught just what to do in this situation: 'When the archer has you in his sight, fly into the sun and use its light'. Follow me!"

To their left, the setting sun had swollen to a bright orange globe. Together Puffin and Odette flew directly into it.

Puffin glanced quickly behind. Derek was shielding his eyes, his bow lowered to his side. They were able to fly like that for about two minutes. Then the sun seemed to flatten against the horizon, and dropped out of sight. Puffin and Odette both gasped. They flew as fast as they could, soaring over the darkening countryside.

On a hill high above the lake, Jean-Bob and Speed looked up into the blue-black sky. The moon was just appearing over the horizon.

"No sign of them yet," Speed remarked.

"I hope zat pudgy Puffin knows what he's doing," Jean-Bob said.

But Speed's eyes were focused on a pair of dots that had risen above the distant treetops.

"They're coming in!" he called out.

Jean-Bob followed his gaze and saw Odette and Puffin, rapidly approaching. As they landed on the rock, all eyes were on the moon. The rising disk now flecked the treetops with white light. Below them, the lake still lay in darkness.

Derek stepped out of the forest, onto the shore of the lake. Bow in hand, he looked around in wonder, taking in the water, the ravaged castle. Hidden on the hill above him, Odette, Puffin, and Jean-Bob watched Derek in silence. Their plan had worked!

"It's almost time, Odette," Puffin said softly.

"Look!"

Moonlight washed over the trees, slowly making its way to the lake.

"I - I can't do it!" Odette cried.

"You have to!" Puffin retorted.

"He'll kill me, Puffin, he'll kill me!"

"If you don't do it now, Odette, you've lost your chance for life!" Puffin replied. "Be brave!"

Puffin's voice was firm. Odette knew she had no choice. She spread her wings and lifted into the sky. Derek turned. His eyes locked onto the swooping white bird. He watched, frozen, as Odette landed

on the lake. Yes, Odette thought, Derek's shock had delayed him. After chasing her so many miles, he hadn't expected her to fly right to him.

The opposite shore was now bathed in moonlight. The light crept closer and closer. Derek lifted his bow to his shoulder. The light was only a few feet from the water now. Odette looked up at the sky. A thick bank of clouds nudged the moon.

"Not now! Not now!" gasped Odette.

Derek tensed his bowstring. Then like a giant hand, the clouds blotted out the moon and the light disappeared on the lake shore.

10

"*CAAAAAAW!*"

Puffin's cry echoed through the forest. He dived from the sky, hitting Derek full-force. The arrow flew wildly into the lake, over Odette's head. Derek and Puffin rolled in the dirt, squawking and shouting. Puffin flapped his wings, smacking the prince, trying to distract him. But Derek seized him and tossed him aside. Springing to his feet, Derek loaded another arrow onto his bow.

Odette thought about flying away, but the clouds were passing. The moon was peering through them, shining dully on the lake shore again. The light inched closer.

Derek held his breath. He aimed his arrow at Odette. This time he would not miss.

Odette closed her eyes. She felt water and light rising around her, shielding her, swirling upward. Then the forest was blotted out by a whirlpool of silver-blue and Derek disappeared from sight. Where was the arrow? Had he shot at her? Odette felt nothing. She was floating now. Soon she couldn't feel any feathers at all.

Then the water and light vanished. Her eyes

blinked open. The first thing she noticed was Derek's face, eyes wide, jaw open with amazement.

Odette smiled, she was on solid ground now. She was human.

"Hello, Derek," she said.

The bow and arrow dropped from Derek's hand. He was transformed, too, from an angry, vengeful hunter to a young man insane with joy. They ran into each other's arms. Derek's embrace took away the pain, the fright, the unbearable gloom of the last day.

"Oh, Odette, I knew you were alive!" Derek said, his voice thick with emotion. "No one believed me, but I knew!"

"Sshhh!" Odette warned him. "You can't stay."

"I didn't mean to shoot at you. I thought you were the Great Animal – " Derek pulled back and looked her in the eye. "Can't stay? No! I'll never let you out of my sight again!"

"Listen to me, Derek – " Odette began.

From the direction of the castle, Rothbart's voice thundered, "Odette!"

"Oh, no!" Odette cried in horror.

"Who is it?" Derek asked. "What's going on?"

"It's him!"

"Who?"

"He has me under a spell!"

"Who does?"

"Odette!" Rothbart called again.

Derek drew his sword. "Let him come! I'll – "

"No!" Odette interrupted. "He has great power! You must go!"

"Then you're coming with me!"

"I can't. When the moon sets, I'll change back into a swan."

"Odette!" The voice was getting closer now.

"Go!" Odette pushed Derek toward the woods.

"There must be some way to break the spell."

"There is," Odette replied. "You must make a vow of everlasting love."

50

"I'll make it! I'll make it," Derek said.

Odette was growing more and more frightened for him.

"You must prove it to the world."

"How?" Derek asked.

"I don't know," said Odette as she frantically shoved him to safety.

Derek turned to leave, then whirled suddenly around. His face was radiant.

"The ball!" he blurted. "Tomorrow night, come to the castle. I will choose you. I will make a vow of everlasting love!"

Tears welled up in Odette's eyes. Derek had risked his life for her. Now he was saying the words she had longed to hear. And for the first time, she felt hope.

"ODETTE!" Rothbart bellowed.

"I'm coming!" Odette shouted back. Then she turned to Derek and whispered, "Go!"

Grabbing one last precious moment, Derek kissed her again. Then he sped away and was swallowed up by the darkness of the forest.

Rothbart crashed through the woods towards her. He glared at her, breathing heavily. His sweaty hair was streaked across his forehead and his skin was red with exertion. He did not look happy.

"Didn't you hear me calling?" he asked.

"I - I -" Odette stammered.

"I thought I heard voices."

Puffin, Jean-Bob, and Speed huddled together in the underbrush, watching the scene. Using his deepest frog-voice, Jean-Bob croaked, "O-dette! O-dette!"

Odette swallowed hard. "Voices?"

"Yes, voices." Rothbart looked over his shoulder.
"Oh . . . er . . . I . . . "

Rothbart stepped toward the woods, peering
intently. Odette panicked. She had to distract him.
"I've decided to become your queen!" she gasped.

Rothbart turned to face her. His eyes were
narrow and wary.

Behind a bush, Jean-Bob fainted at the news.

Rothbart's voice was hushed and awestruck.

"You mean – Oh, Odette, you've made me so
happy!" He took her hand and kneeled. With that,
he got up and walked back toward the castle.

"Oh, by the way," Rothbart said, turning back,
"you wouldn't happen to know who this belongs to,
would you?" From the folds of his cape, Rothbart
took out a bow, Derek's bow.

Odette felt herself growing numb.

" 'Come to the ball! I will make a vow of
everlasting love!'" Rothbart threw his head back
and cackled. With a mighty swing of his arm he
threw the bow far into the lake. "Thought you
could fool Rothbart, did you?"

"I will never be yours, you vile creature!" Odette
shot back. "I will marry Prince Derek, and you
cannot stop me!"

Rothbart's face turned red. His lips pulled back over his teeth like an angry animal. He grabbed her arms with all his strength. But Odette had no fear. She locked eyes with him. At moonrise tomorrow she would be human again and Rothbart would be powerless against her. Tomorrow she would be free.

Rothbart took a deep breath and let go of Odette. His snarl vanished and he chuckled.

"I hate to tell you this, Odette, but you won't be able to attend the ball tomorrow night."

"If you want to stop me," Odette replied, "you'll have to kill me."

"I don't think so. You see, you've forgotten one very important thing."

Rothbart's smile chilled Odette to the bone.

"Tomorrow," he said, "there is no moon."

With that, Rothbart strolled back to his castle, laughing triumphantly.

11

The Hag cackled with laughter as Rothbart told her what had just happened.

"No matter what they do," he declared, "I'm always one step ahead!"

Then Rothbart suddenly grew serious. "On the other hand, Prince Derek's vow could ruin everything."

The Hag nodded.

"I'm going to have to deal with him," Rothbart said, pacing up and down. "But how?"

The Hag shrugged.

"The vow!" Rothbart said. "I'll get Derek to offer his vow to the wrong princess!"

The Hag looked confused.

"Don't you see?" Rothbart asked. "I'll make you look like Odette!"

Slowly the idea sank in. The Hag gave Rothbart a huge, gap-toothed smile.

"It's going to take a lot of work but it'll be worth it, because when Derek makes his vow to the wrong girl, Odette will die! Then I'll finish him off myself." He laughed again. "Oh, I love it!"

At sunrise the next day, Queen Uberta's castle sprang to life. Servants swarmed in and out, cleaning, dusting, washing and trimming. Candles were replaced, carpets were beaten and mirrors polished. Every crystal on every chandelier had to sparkle like a diamond. In the ballroom, Lord Rogers and his musicians prepared for a rehearsal, while Uberta busily inspected the flower arrangements. Derek suddenly swept in.

"Oh, Derek, there you are," Uberta said.

"What are these?" Derek asked, gesturing to a bouquet.

Uberta looked at him oddly. "Roses."

"They're red."

"Of course they're red!"

"But, Mother, I don't want red roses. I want white, like a swan."

"White roses? Whatever for?"

"Because white is pure. It's delicate, like a – a swan."

"A swan," Uberta repeated dryly.

The orchestra under Lord Rogers had just begun thumping out a loud waltz.

"No, no, no!" Derek shouted. "Hold it!"

Lord Rogers turned from the conductor's podium as the players stopped. Queen Uberta looked at her son as if he had lost his mind.

"What's wrong?" Rogers asked.

"Everything," Derek replied. "It's all wrong. Tonight the music must be played with feeling, softly, gracefully, like a swan. Have you ever seen a swan, Rogers?"

"Of course I've seen a swan."

"If you could play a swan, what would it sound like?"

Rogers smiled. "Honking."

"Soft and graceful, Rogers," Derek said sternly.

Then he turned to survey the room. "Where's Bromley?"

"No one has seen him, Derek," Uberta replied.

"You're kidding. Who's going to be my best man?"

"Best . . . " Uberta was almost shocked speechless.

"You mean you . . ."

Derek gave his mother a wink as the orchestra swung into a lilting ballad.

"There you go, Rogers!" Derek called out. "That's the stuff!"

He hopped on to the podium, took the baton from Rogers, and began conducting himself. "That's it! That's it!" he cried, then handing the baton back to Rogers, he leaped off the platform and danced, alone, grinning wildly and holding his arms out as if he had a partner. Around the room, everyone stopped and stared.

"Come on, Mother!" Prince Derek swept Queen Uberta into his arms.

Uberta laughed as they danced across the room.

"Don't be so secretive, Derek," she urged. "Tell me who it is!"

Laughing, Derek took Uberta's roses and flung them high in the air. His secret would keep until later that night.

Long-stemmed roses splashed into the warm, foul water around Odette. High in the dank water dungeon tower, Rothbart hung out of an opening that led into his castle, dropping roses into the water.

"Hurts me deeply," he sighed, "but then, a king has to do what a king has to do."

Odette hated being confined in this dark, horrible place. Angrily she picked up a rose with her beak and snapped it in two.

"Now then, you're getting cross again," Rothbart mocked. Odette swam sullenly around.

"Well, I can't leave you like this," Rothbart went on. "If you're not happy, I'm not happy." He thought a minute, then snapped his fingers.

"I know! If you can't attend the ball, I'll bring the ball to you! Let's see . . . The first thing you'll need is a young man. The prince is busy, of course, but I think I can arrange a substitute."

Odette looked up. She could hear grunts and

scuffling from a door next to Rothbart. Into the opening stepped Bromley!

"The poor fellow got lost in the woods," Rothbart said.

The Hag planted her foot on Bromley's backside and pushed.

"No!" Bromley teetered at the edge, his arms going round like windmills. Then, shrieking, he fell, and with a hugh splash, he plunged into the water.

Odette swam to him as fast as she could. His head bobbed up and he flailed about crazily.

"Help! I can't swim!" he shouted.

Odette bit onto his shirt and pulled him to the dungeon wall. There he grabbed onto the jagged edge of one of the stones.

"Don't leave me here!" Bromley cried.

"I'd love to stay," Rothbart replied, "but if I don't leave now, I'll be late for the ball, and that would be rude."

He gave Odette a sharp, angry glare. "Don't give me that look, Missy. You had to drag your weakling prince into it, didn't you? Well, that's fine by me!"

Rothbart disappeared into the castle. His cackling filtered into the water dungeon. Mixed with Bromley's sobs it made Odette's blood run cold.

12

The chamberlain burst into the royal dressing room.

"Excuse me, Your Highness. It's getting rather crowded outside."

Queen Uberta rose from her seat.

"Very well. You may begin the introductions and, Chamberlain, no mistakes this time. Everything must be perfect."

"Oh, yes, Ma'am. Perfect."

He dashed out of the door, tightly holding his stack of invitations.

Uberta turned to Derek, who was buttoning his shirtsleeves.

"Promise me, Derek, that you'll tell me who it is the moment she arrives."

"Don't worry, Mother, you'll know," Derek replied. "Believe me, you'll know."

Puffin paced outside the Water Dungeon, deep in thought. "It's coming," he muttered.

Jean-Bob and Speed watched him patiently.

"What is?" Jean-Bob asked.

"An idea," Puffin answered. "A substantial idea. A large, colossal idea."

"Sounds big," Speed said.

Puffin stopped walking, his eyes growing large.

"I've got it! Water leaks into the dungeon, right? Well, if there's a leak, there must be a hole. And if there's a hole . . ."

"If zere's a hole," Jean-Bob said, "Odette would've come out already."

"Not if it was a very tiny hole," Puffin countered. "We'll find the hole, make it bigger, and pull her out!"

"I think you're forgetting something." Jean-Bob opened his mouth and snapped it shut, imitating an alligator.

"His Majesty's got a point," Speed said.

"Not to worry, Puffin's in charge!" Puffin

announced. "Okay, first we need a scout."

"Are you crazy?" Jean-Bob said. "Who are you going to find to jump into zis moat?"

Puffin looked at Jean-Bob. "He's got to be a good swimmer."

"I should say so!" Jean-Bob declared.

"He's got to be small, too," Speed suggested.

"Tiny," Jean-Bob agreed. "Not to be seen!"

"And it wouldn't hurt if he were green," Puffin continued, "for camouflage purposes."

"Precisely! Small, good swimmer, green . . ." Jean-Bob stopped in mid-sentence. "Good grief! Are you talking about me?"

Puffin began pacing again. "Now, the first thing we'll do is create a diversion."

"No! Stop it!" Jean-Bob protested. "Absolutely not!"

"That's where you come into play, Jean-Bob," Puffin went on.

"I can't hear you!" Jean-Bob cried.

Puffin calmly put his wing around Jean-Bob and pulled the frog close. "Now, here's what I want you to do. . . ."

The chamberlain shut the heavy oak door to the castle ballroom. Every princess had arrived. He

63

had counted them all carefully. With a smile, he descended the grand staircase. The princesses stood about, each lovelier than the one next to her. Bedecked with jewels, they outshone the brilliant chandeliers. One by one, they danced with Derek to the strains of the royal orchestra.

It was perfect. Just as the queen had requested. The chamberlain held his chin high.

Finally, after the last dance, Queen Uberta approached her son.

"Well, Derek?" she asked expectantly.

Boom! Boom! Boom!

The chamberlain jumped. Who could be knocking at the ballroom door now? Queen Uberta scowled at him.

"Chamberlain? All who were invited are present, are they not?"

The chamberlain's hands shook as he looked through the invitations. "I - I - Yes! I mean, Katherine of Tearean, Anne of Wilshire, yes, I'm sure that – "

Boom! Boom! Boom!

The queen's face was reddening with rage.

"I certainly hope that you have not locked anyone out."

"Me, too," the chamberlain said with a gulp. He ran up the steps and pulled the door open. The entire ballroom fell silent. Derek stared in awe.

A princess walked into the light. Her beauty made all the others look plain. Her gown shimmered, throwing a radiant halo around her.

"She's made it," Derek said to himself with rising ecstasy. "Odette's made it, and this time I won't let her leave."

Smiling and thrilled that the disguise was working, the Hag slowly walked down the stairs.

13

"It can't be," Queen Uberta said under her breath.

Derek moved toward the stairs. Around him, the guests murmured in disbelief.

Uberta leaned toward the podium.

"Rogers! Who is it? Do you know her?"

"I . . . don't know," Rogers said hesitantly.

"Come now, Rogers," Uberta said. "I know he confides in you. Who is it?"

"I promise, I do not know her. Although she does look a great deal like – "

"But it couldn't be!" Queen Uberta squinted at the young lady, whose face so resembled the poor, dead daughter of King William. "Could it?"

Derek approached his beloved. He reached out and touched her soft cheek.

"I was so worried," he said, beaming. "I almost thought – "

"Nothing could keep me away," the Hag replied.

Derek turned to Lord Rogers and snapped his fingers twice. Immediately Rogers signalled to the orchestra, and as Derek's tune filled the ballroom, the prince began to dance with the girl of his dreams.

A few yards from the moat, Puffin rubbed Jean-Bob's shoulders.

"Okay. Speed will draw the 'gators away. Then you'll get a running start and go for that hole."

"If I can find it," Jean-Bob said nervously, "And if ze alligators don't chew me before I get zere!"

"Don't worry," Puffin assured him, "Speed will rush to help."

Puffin raised his wing high. Across the moat, Speed waited for his signal.

"On your mark!" Puffin bellowed.

Jean-Bob shook out his legs and crouched into a sprinter's position. Speed began shouting at the alligators.

"Hey, you old leatherheads, come and get me! Come on, bulbous eyes! This way, chicken lips!"

The alligators turned. They floated angrily toward Speed.

"Perfect!" Puffin said. "Okay, ready . . . steady . . . go!"

Jean-Bob bounded toward the moat.

"Faster!" Puffin urged. "Faster!"

Higher and higher Jean-Bob leaped. "Sure," he muttered to himself. "Go on, Jean-Bob, race to your death!"

The alligators were floating in Speed's direction.
Their backs were turned to Jean-Bob. But not for
long. One of them looked back for a moment. His
eyes met Jean-Bob's. Instantly he turned. Jean-Bob
tried to pull up short, but he was going too fast.
With a terrified scream, he bounced into the water.
When he rose to the surface, he was
looking into the eyes of two hungry alligators.

"Aaagh!" he shrieked, and began swimming for his life.

Speed whizzed by him. "Get moving, slowcoach!" he called to Jean-Bob.

"Slowcoach?" Jean-Bob said.

The alligators tore past him, intent on catching Speed.

So that was how the turtle got his nickname! Jean-Bob dived underwater. He swam to the wall of the water dungeon. He examined it, block by block. Where was the opening?

"Any luck?" came Speed's voice.

Jean-Bob looked around. Before he could answer, a wall of alligators swam into view. Speed darted out of the way. But this time, the alligators didn't go after him. They headed straight for Jean-Bob, who had no time to think. If he didn't do something drastic he was dinner without a doubt. He could barely see the hole, but there it was, impossibly small, leaking between two loose stones at the base of the tower.

Thrusting out his legs, he shot into the tiny opening. Halfway in, he twisted and turned, but his body only jammed tighter and tighter.

He was stuck!

14

With all his strength, Jean-Bob inched his body
further and further inward. His legs disappeared
into the hole. An alligator lunged after him and
crashed into the tower wall. The impact shook the
tower. Stones broke loose. Jean-Bob blasted like a
rocket through the wall. He shot through the water
inside the tower, and straight up above the surface.

Hanging over the water was a rusted iron ring.
Jean-Bob grabbed it and hung on.

"Jean-Bob!" cried Odette, floating below him.

Jean-Bob smiled weakly. "To the rescue,
mademoiselle!"

Outside the tower, Puffin stood on a tree branch
and watched. Speed was still leading the alligators
around the tower. Suddenly the turtle rose into the
air and spun.

"There's the signal," Puffin said to himself. "All
right, Puffin, time to brush up on diving
technique."

He launched himself downward. When he rose to
the surface, the alligators were staring at him.

"How about a little white meat?" Puffin taunted.

"Good for the heart!"

As the alligators chased Puffin, Speed plunged downward. He found Jean-Bob's hole and began digging. Yes! The alligators had loosened the stones. Speed began clearing them away with his claws. The hole widened quickly.

From his hanging ring, Jean-Bob leaped into the water. He dived to the hole, spotted Speed pushing away the stones, and raced to the surface.

"We've broken through!" he called to Odette.

"Oh, Jean-Bob, thank you!" Odette replied.

"When all this is over, remind me to give you a kiss."

Jean-Bob beamed.

Odette swam to Bromley. She knew she would face one big problem - humans could not understand animal speech.

She grabbed his shirt with her bill and pulled.

"What? What is it?" Bromley said, his eyes wide with fright. "Stay away! What are you doing? No! Go away!"

71

Odette let go. She stared at him. He was Derek's best friend but he was frozen with fear. She had no time to waste. She plunged into the water and swam hard. Speed saw her and held up a hand.

"I'll tell you when," he said.

He stuck his head out of the hole just as Puffin's webbed feet swam by – followed by madly paddling alligator legs.

Speed looked back to Odette. "Let's go!"

He squeezed out. Odette followed close behind. The first thing she saw as she emerged was a pair of eyes, yellow and hungry, and a gaping mouth full of pointed teeth! Odette ducked back into the hole as the alligator bit down.

That was close! She shot out of the hole. With a powerful leg thrust, she swam for the surface.

Now another alligator was after her. She pulled away, losing a few feathers. Speed lurched into action, knocking one alligator away. Odette splashed through the surface. Behind her rose another alligator, jaws wide, ready to close around her. Beside him rose Puffin. Hunching his body, he struck at the alligator with his webbed feet. The alligator fell back into the moat.

Odette, throwing off water in a jet stream, took to the air!

15

Derek and his princess swirled around the ballroom. The other guests stared enviously, and Queen Uberta was sobbing with joy.

Derek looked deeply into the eyes of Odette's double. Their blue colour was as deep as he remembered. Her hair shone like firelight, just as before. She was perfect, almost. A moment earlier, he had been dizzy with happiness. But that had faded. Something wasn't right. Derek managed a shy smile.

"Odette, you seem . . . I don't know, different," he said.

The Hag smiled. From inside her gown, she pulled out a locket, the locket Prince Derek had given Odette as a child. "Don't worry," she reassured him. "After tonight, everything will be perfect."

Derek fingered the old locket. Odette had kept it close to her, always. She must truly love him. How could he have doubted her?

As the couple danced near the orchestra, Derek tapped Lord Rogers on the shoulder.

"Rogers," he said, "I have an announcement to make."

With an obedient nod, Rogers stopped the music and the guests applauded politely as Derek bowed to his partner. He took her hand and squeezed it gently. Then he led her up the red-carpeted ballroom stairs.

The guests watched, whispering in anticipation. Queen Uberta wiped tears from her eyes. A few of the other princesses could not disguise the envy in their eyes. At the top of the stairs, Derek turned. He raised his arms, quieting the crowd's murmur.

"Kings and Queens, Princes and Princesses, Ladies and Gentlemen!" he called out. "And, of course, Mother."

Uberta smiled and dabbed her cheek with a handkerchief.

"I have an announcement to make," Derek went on. "Today I have found my bride."

Outside the ballroom window, under the moonless sky, Odette hovered, panting for breath. It couldn't be true. Derek was holding another girl's hand! He was announcing his engagement!

"No," she whispered.

She began to batter at the window with her tired wings.

"No, Derek!" she cried. "It's a trick!"

No one could hear her.

"And now," Derek was saying, "before the whole world, I make a vow to break all vows . . ."

Odette flew to a closer window and banged frantically again.

"No! Derek! Over here! Derek!"

From window to window Odette flew, trying to attract Derek's attention, but all eyes were on the prince and his love.

". . . a vow," Derek continued, "that is stronger than all the powers on earth."

"DEREK, PLEASE!" Odette was right above him now, desperate for him to hear her. "DON'T DO IT! IT'S A TRICK! DEREK!"

"I make a vow of everlasting love . . ." Derek turned to the imposter with a rapturous smile, ". . . to Odette!"

The applause was instant. The castle seemed to explode from within. And so did Odette's heart. She hovered, staring in shock. Derek had declared his love to someone else. Odette would remain forever a swan, forever loveless. She raised her head skyward. An anguished cry welled up from the depths of her imprisoned body. And then she went limp, falling to the earth.

16

Above Derek, a window smashed open. Around the ballroom, one by one, the other windows swung inward. An icy wind whipped through the room. Screams rang out. Bewildered, Derek looked around. The ballroom door flew open. Against the inky darkness, his cape billowing in the wind, stood Rothbart.

"Hello, Little Prince."

Derek held his ground. He stood face-to-face with Rothbart.

"Who are you?" he asked defiantly.

Rothbart cackled. "Went and pledged your love to another, eh?"

"What are you talking about? This is Odette!"

"No," Rothbart replied. "Odette is mine."

Now Derek knew who this stranger was. Only one person could make that claim. Only the Enchanter who had attacked King William and cast the spell on his princess.

"You!" Derek said. "You're powerless here. I've made a vow, a vow of everlasting love!"

"You've made a vow all right," Rothbart mocked. "A vow of everlasting death!"

Rothbart raised his right arm and sent forth a blast of harsh light. It hit Derek's beautiful partner, spreading over her entire body. The guests gasped in horror.

"No!" Derek shouted.

The young princess fell to the ground, head down. Derek ran to her. He cradled her in his arms, lifting her head, turning her to see if her face showed signs of life. Her blond hair fell over his arms. He found himself staring into the thick, warty face of the grinning, foul-breathed Hag!

Derek jumped to his feet. Odette! Where was Odette?

"You should have left her to me!" cried Rothbart. "Now Odette will die!"

Suddenly the Hag shrieked, pointing to a window. Derek turned to look. In the receding glow of the ballroom light, a dim white form flew slowly away from the castle.

A swan.

"Odette," Derek said, his voice choking and weak. His feet propelled him out of the castle door. He turned in the direction of the swan and shouted, "ODETTE!"

The white form was gone.

17

Derek ran to the stable and mounted his horse.

"If you hurry, Little Prince," Rothbart called from the castle door, "I'll let you see her one last time!"

But Derek was not listening.

"Odette!" he cried once more, urging his horse into a gallop.

The sharp wind tore against him as he rode across the castle lawn. The horse sped blindly into the forest, its feet barely touching the ground. The trees loomed around Derek, black and dense. Through eyes narrowed against the blinding gale,

79

he manoeuvred his horse around them. All the while he shouted the name of his beloved. Not once did she answer. Not once did the swan appear overhead. Deep in the woods, the trees seemed to crowd in. The horse faltered. She began to buck and shy, whinnying in fear. Derek drew his sword and dismounted. Alone, on foot, he cut through the undergrowth.

"She's fading fast!" Rothbart's voice floated in the air like an evil spirit.

"No!" Derek shouted, slashing right and left.

Inside the water dungeon, Bromley clung to the small ledge, whimpering. He had heard the voice, too. Rothbart was getting closer. The last place he wanted to be was in this stinking tower. Slowly he released his fingers from the rock and dived into the water.

Outside, Jean-Bob, Speed, and Puffin stood near the lake, looking upward.

"Something's gone wrong," Puffin said.

"Zere she is!" Jean-Bob shouted.

Barely clearing the treetops, Odette flew toward them. Her wings flapped slowly and her body hung limp.

"I don't think she's going to make it," Speed remarked.

"This way, Odette!" Puffin shouted. "Just a little further!"

Jean-Bob and Speed joined the shouting. Odette lifted her head a little. She tried to slow herself down and level out, but she could not stop herself from plummeting downwards. She swooped over their heads and crashed onto the stone floor by the lake. The animals gathered around her motionless body.

"Is she still alive?" gasped Speed.

"I don't know," the horrified Puffin replied.

Jean-Bob leaned over her. "Please, Odette. Don't die."

The swan's dull white form began to change. A flicker of light appeared, seeming to come from within. Then the light radiated outward, growing into a bright wash of yellow and white and orange and blue. Jean-Bob, Speed, and Puffin moved back and watched. When the light receded, the swan was gone. Now Odette the princess was lying on the stone.

At the edge of the woods, Derek emerged from the thick darkness. He stopped for a moment, panting, hardly able to stand. The animals looked at him sadly. None of them was able to say a word. Derek glanced around and saw Odette. With new strength, he sprinted to her side and dropped to his knees.

"Odette," he said, lifting her head into his chest. "What have I done to you? Forgive me, Odette, forgive me."

Hearing his voice, Odette stirred. She struggled to open her eyes.

"Derek – " Her voice was almost lost to the wind.

Derek looked into her face with new hope, trying to catch her gaze.

"I feel so weak." Odette murmured. "I think . . ."

"No, you'll live, Odette!" Derek stroked her hair tenderly, supporting her with his strong arms. "It's you I love. It's you! The vow I made was for you."

Derek set Odette down gently. He stood up and raised his despairing eyes to the heavens, to wherever Rothbart might be.

"I made the vow for her! Do you hear?" he shouted. "THE VOW I MADE WAS FOR HER!"

From behind him came a soft, grating voice.

"No need to shout."

Derek snapped around to face Rothbart.

"Don't let her die!" he pleaded.

Rothbart smiled. "Is that a threat?"

Derek stepped forward and grabbed the Enchanter by his cloak.

"Don't you dare let her die," he hissed.

"Ah, it is a threat," Rothbart replied.

"You're the only one with the power. Make her better!"

"Only if you defeat me," laughed Rothbart.

A wave of his arm sent a blaze of light into the night air. It wrapped around Rothbart, pulsing and glowing. A blinding flash made Derek reel backward. When he looked up, Rothbart was a towering, snarling beast. It was the Great Animal. The creature bellowed so loudly that the trees seemed to bend.

Cowering behind a rock, Jean-Bob said to Speed and Puffin, "I'm betting on the animal."

"I won't let her die!" Derek shouted. He picked up his sword and ran it into the beast. The Great Animal snarled. As if plucking a small weed, it lifted Derek off the ground, then tossed him down the stone stairs that led to the lake.

Derek's sword flew out of his hand as he landed in the shallow water's edge. Before he could stand, the Great Animal attacked again. Derek struggled to his feet. He clamped his hands around the creature's neck and tried to squeeze. With its massive beak, it tore into Derek's shoulder.

"Odette!" Derek yelled, falling to the ground.

The Great Animal leaped up into the air, then landed on Derek, grabbing him in its talons.

Behind the rock, Puffin suddenly shouted to his cohorts, "The bow! Swim to the bottom of the lake and get the bow!"

Puffin grabbed Speed and hurled him into the lake. Jean-Bob jumped in after him.

Above them soared the Great Animal with Derek in its clutches. Crying out in triumph, it flung Derek into a sturdy pine tree. With a sickening thump, Derek smashed against it and tumbled to the forest floor. He tried to stand. Grimacing in pain, he fell unconscious.

At the bottom of the lake, Jean-Bob saw the bow stuck in a tangle of weeds. He pulled frantically, but it wouldn't move. In an instant, Speed was by his side. Together they yanked once, twice, till the bow jerked upward, out of the mud. Speed took it and swam to the water's surface. Jean-Bob, still holding the bow, was dragged along with him. As their faces broke through the surface, they looked for Derek.

He lay limp on the ground as the Great Animal circled above him, ready to descend for the kill.

18

"Throw it!" Puffin shouted. "Throw it!"

Speed reared back and threw. Still clutching the
bow, Jean-Bob went flying with it. With a jolt, bow
and frog landed on the forest floor near Derek.
Jean-Bob jumped on to the prince's head.

"Wake up!" he said, lifting Derek's eyelids.
"Hello?"

The shadow of the Great Animal grew larger
around them.

"Good-bye," Jean-Bob said with a gulp and he
leaped out of the way.

But Derek was stirring. He opened his eyes. The claws of the Great Animal were dropping toward him fast. Quickly he grabbed the bow. He reached over his back for an arrow. And then he realized he wasn't carrying any.

"Oh, please, please, please . . ." piped up a small voice near the water dungeon.

"Brom?" Derek said.

Soaking wet, Bromley stood just outside the tower. He aimed at Derek's chest with his bow and arrow.

"NOW!" Bromley shouted.

Bromley released his arrow. It sliced through the air. Derek spun round and with a snap of his wrist, he snatched the arrow out of the air. Loading it onto his bow, he pointed it upward.

The Great Animal stopped in mid flight. Its evil yellow eyes whitened with fear as Derek let fly. The arrow shot upward and planted itself in the creature's chest. A great howl swept over the lake like a tornado. The beast seemed to hover, suspended in the air like an awful, misshapen balloon. Then, slowly, it dropped into the lake.

For a moment, there was silence. Not even a rustling leaf could be heard. Then the Great Animal floated to the surface, dead. The silence was broken by Jean-Bob, Puffin, and Speed.

"Hurrah!" they shouted.

Bromley stood on the opposite shore, his mouth hanging open. But Derek took no joy in his kill. He leaned over the lifeless body of his princess, the only true love of his life, the love he had given up, the love that had blinded him to the evil trick of Rothbart. Quietly weeping, he gathered Odette's body in his arms.

"Forgive me, Odette. I only wanted to break the spell. To prove my love." He choked back a sob. "I'll always love you."

The words seemed to float from his lips and bathe the dead princess. Colour flowed into the ghostly white skin of her face. She felt lighter in Derek's arms. And then, she moved. Derek pushed her matted hair from her forehead. Could it be? Slowly Princess Odette opened her eyes.

"Oh, Derek!" she said, her voice faint.

"Odette!" Derek shouted.

Her arms closed around him. And he held her with all the strength and joy in his overflowing heart.

The animals turned to one another, trying not to cry.

"Well," Puffin said. "There you have it. Everlasting love."

19

The bells of the royal cathedral had not rung as loudly in years. Every house in the kingdom was empty. No one would miss the wedding of Prince Derek to Princess Odette. They filled the cathedral, spilling into the streets. Never before had a noise been heard like the roar that greeted the young husband and wife as they burst through the church door. The hats thrown joyously into the air created a momentary eclipse of the sun.

Lord Rogers and Bromley stood outside the church, watching the pandemonium.

"Well, Rogers, old man," Bromley remarked, "I suppose you owe me an apology. After all, if it weren't for me, the Great Animal would still be alive."

Behind Rogers's head, the shadow of a winged beast appeared on the wall. Bromley's eyes widened as it loomed larger and larger.

"Dear me," Rogers gasped, staring at something over Bromley's shoulder. "No!"

"Wh – what is it?" Bromley stammered.

"The Great Animal! It's alive!"

With a terrified cry, Bromley fainted to the floor.

Queen Uberta passed by Rogers, her elaborate swan wig balanced regally on top of her head. Rogers chuckled to himself. How fortunate the wig's shadow looked so gruesome.

"Uberta," he said with a grin.

"Rogers," Uberta replied warmly.

A few hours later, the reception at the new palace began. Derek and Odette marvelled at how fast the queen's subjects had renovated Rothbart's castle. Now it stood proudly over the water, scrubbed and inviting. For now it belonged to the prince and princess. Above them swooped the new Royal Air Force - General Puffin and his army of swans!

As the party went on noisily inside, Odette stood near the lake with Jean-Bob and Speed. Jean-Bob looked up at the princess, leaning his cheek towards her. He wore a small, velvet cape and a crown.

"Don't be too disappointed, Jean-Bob, if nothing happens," Odette warned.

Jean-Bob ignored her.

"Finally, after all zese years," he said, "I shall return to my throne!"

"Don't forget to write," Speed said.

Jean-Bob glowered at him.

"You still don't believe me, do you?"

"The only thing you're going to turn is red," Speed replied.

Jean-Bob looked defiantly at Odette.

"I'm ready," he said.

Odette leaned over and planted a gentle kiss on his cheek. Jean-Bob spun around. His eyes rolled. He gasped. He doubled over, covering his face. Then, triumphantly, he raised himself to his full height.

He looked exactly the same.

"Ha!" he cried. "What do you have to say now, Speed?"

"Er . . ." Speed began.

"Zat's what I thought!" Jean-Bob said. "And now,

if you don't mind, I have some socializing to do!"

He threw his cape over his shoulder and strolled into the crowd. With a princely swagger he nodded to the guests.

"Bonjour, madame. How are you today, sir? Hello, my little flower."

The young maiden screamed and fainted at the sight of a frog.

"Ha! I can still make zem swoon!" Jean-Bob gloated.

As he disappeared into the party, Odette smiled at Speed.

"Would you like a kiss, too?"

"No thanks," Speed answered. "I'm quite happy as a turtle."

From behind them, Derek called out, "There you are!"

Odette turned to her prince. He was smiling at her from the entrance to the castle.

"There are still a hundred people waiting to see you inside," he said.

Odette sighed. "Well, I suppose there's only one thing we can do."

They looked at each other for a moment, then broke into wide smiles. Laughing, they took each other's hands and ran away from their new home.

In the clear glow of the moonlight, they glided across the vast lawn. They stopped only when they reached the new bridge that spanned the lake.

Derek twirled his bride in the air. As he set her down gently, she gazed into his eyes. Below them, the lake lapped against the shore. In the distance, music and merry laughter rang out from the castle windows.

"Will you love me, Derek," Princess Odette asked, "until the day I die?"

"No," Derek replied. "Much longer than that, Odette, much longer."

As he took her in his arms and kissed her, Odette knew in her heart it was a promise that would last forever.